published by

NATIONAL CENTER for
YOUTH ISSUES

www.ncyi.org

To my mom for always being there for me. I love you!

– Julia Cook

To my three little verbs, Sophia, Abigail, & Jack.

– Carrie Hartman

NATIONAL CENTER for
YOUTH ISSUES

P.O. Box 22185 • Chattanooga, TN 37422-2185
423.899.5714 • 866.318.6294 • fax: 423.899.4547
www.ncyi.org

ISBN: 978-1-931636-84-1 $9.95 Softcover

Written by: Julia Cook
Illustrations by: Carrie Hartman
Design by: Phillip W. Rodgers
Contributing Editor: Jennifer Deshler

Published by National Center for Youth Issues
Softcover

Printed at RR Donnelley
Reynosa, Tamaulipas, Mexico • May 2018

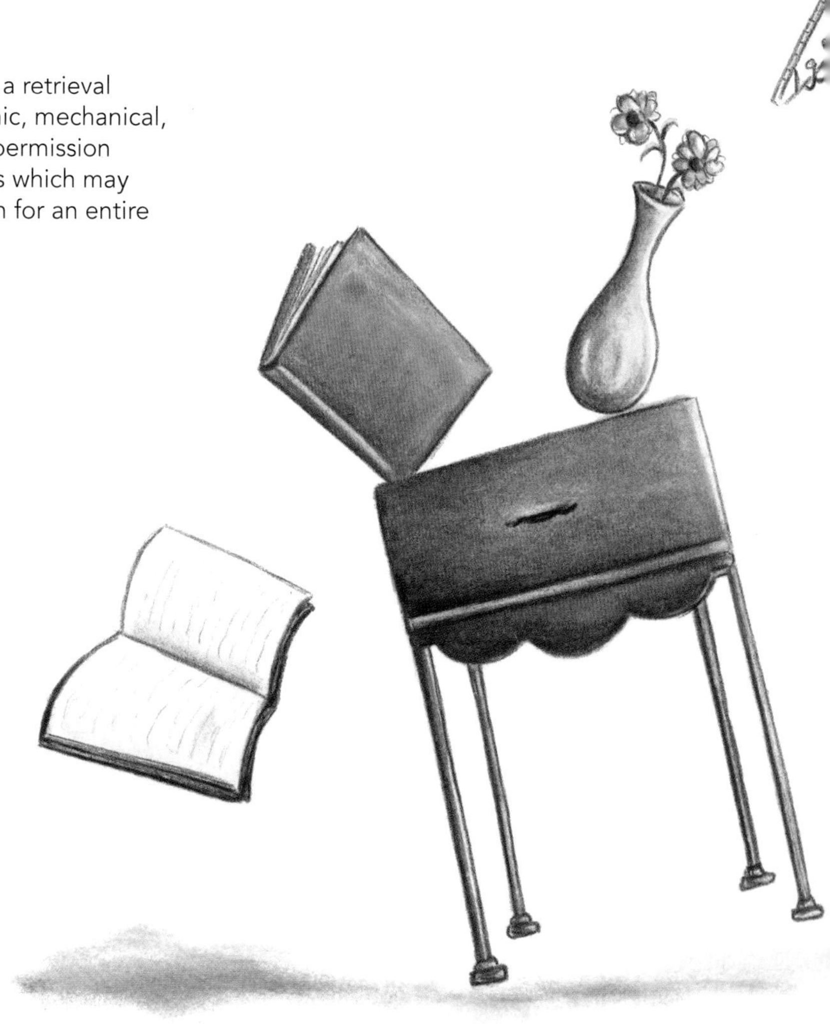

My name is Louis.

People say I am a verb.

That's because I'm always doing something.

The problem is that most of the time,
I end up doing the wrong "something."

It's hard to be a verb!

My knees start **itching.**

My toes start **twitching.**

My skin gets **jumpy.**

Others get **grumpy.**

When it comes to sitting still.

It's just not my deal.

Haven't you heard?

I am a

VERB!

Look Sassy
Look Cool

Last week, my mom took me to get my hair cut.
She told me I had to sit really, really still.
I did at first, and then...

My knees started **itching.**

My toes started **twitching.**

My skin got **jumpy.**

The lady got **grumpy.**

She went to make a cut,
but I moved and guess what?
She made a hole in my hair
that looked just like a pear.

"Sit still, Louis!" my mom said.

"My sitter is still," I said.
"It's my feet that are moving!"
"It's hard to be a verb!," I told my mom.

"You just have to focus," she said.

At school, we have to sit in our desks during work time. Work time lasts for 30 minutes. To me, it seems like it lasts for 16 years!

It's hard for me to stay at my desk.

The other day, I started out doing just fine and then I saw a brand new poster hanging up on the wall across the room.

My knees started **itching.**

My toes started **twitching.**

My skin got **jumpy.**

My teacher got **grumpy.**

I got out of my seat, and I tried out my feet.

"Sit down, Louis!," said my teacher.

"Go back to your seat!"

"It's hard to be a verb!," I told her.

"You just have to focus," she said.

When I have to get ready for school in the morning, it seems like it takes me forever!

Every morning, my mom has to tell me the exact same thing over and over and over again:

"Get out of bed, Louis."

"Get dressed, Louis."

"You're gonna be late for school..."

Eat breakfast, Louis.

Wash your face, Louis.

"You're gonna be late for school..."

Brush your teeth, Louis.

Comb your hair, Louis.

"You're gonna be late for school..."

Feed the dog, Louis.

Let him out, Louis.

"You're gonna be late for school..."

A few days ago...

I got out of bed just fine and then I got dressed... well, almost.

While I was eating my breakfast, I saw my brand new football sitting there on the floor.

My knees started **itching.**
My toes started **twitching.**

I picked up my ball, and...

threw it
against the wall!

My skin got **jumpy.**

My mom got **grumpy.**

Playing with the ball made no sense at all.

"Louis!" my mom said.
"You need to focus!"

I forgot to brush my teeth. **But I did** feed the dog.

I forgot to comb my hair. **But I did** wash my face.

I made it to school on time.
But when I came home that afternoon,
I realized something...

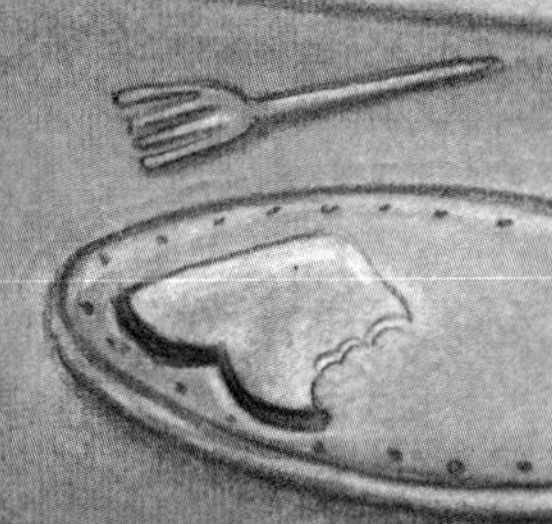

I forgot to let out my dog!

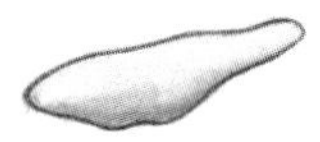

"LOUIS!!!!" my mom said in a not-so-nice voice, "Something has to change!"

"You have got to learn to FOCUS!

There are two time-frames in life: 'NOW' and 'NOT NOW.'
And to you 'NOT NOW' never seems to matter!"

"OOOOPS," I said. "I'm sorry mom. I guess I just forgot."

It's so hard to be a verb......

My knees start **itching.**

My toes start **twitching.**

I forget a lot of stuff. My life is so rough. I make people mad, and then I feel bad.

I know it sounds strange. Oh how I wish I could change."

"You can change," said my mom. "All you have to do is learn how to focus."

"I try and I try," I said to my mom. "But I just can't do it."

"I think I know how to help you," said my mom.

"First of all, whenever you know you are going to have to sit still for a while, wiggle your wiggles before they wiggle you."

"What does that mean?" I asked.

"Scratch your knees.
Wiggle your toes.
Stretch your skin.
Crinkle your nose."

"Shake your elbows.
Bend at the waist.
Dance in a circle,
And scrunch up your face!"

"You be in charge of all wiggles at large."

"Wiggle them first so they can't make you BURST!"

Mom showed me how to wiggle my wiggles.

We even did a wiggle dance.

My dad said we both looked very, very strange.

"Next, we need to find you a '**Focus Squishy**,'" said my mom.

"A what?" I asked.

"A Focus Squishy," she said.

"It's a soft little something
you hold in your hand.

No one else knows you have it,
they might not understand."

You can wiggle your fingers,
while you listen and learn.

"It will help you sit still until
it's your turn."

My mom got out my dad's tackle box and found a shiny, glittery, rubbery worm.

She cut the worm in half and gave me a piece. We practiced using our Focus Squishies. My dad said what we were doing was very, very strange.

"Finally," she said, "I need to make you a **Nag Board**."

"A what?" I asked.

"A Nag Board. Every morning I have to tell you what to do to get ready for school. I end up telling you over and over and over again!"

"**A Nag Board is a list** of all of those things."

"You can even check them off as you do them, and I won't have to nag you as much."

"All I will have to say to you is, 'Louis, check your list.'"

We went to the store and my mom bought a dry erase marker board. We brought it home and she wrote "Nag Board" at the top, then listed everything I need to do before school.

My dad read the "Nag Board."
He thought it was very, very strange.

LOUIS'S
NAG BOARD
- Get out of bed on time

Today, I used all of my new tricks and guess what? They really worked! I got everything done on my Nag Board, and I was on time for school!

I wiggled my wiggles before story time and they didn't end up wiggling me. And, I used my Focus Squishy without anyone knowing about it and...

I got a STAR for being a good listener.

"How's my little verb?" my mom asked as I came through the door.

"Fantastic," I said as I sat on the floor.

"I had a great day and I did everything right.

My teacher was nice and we didn't fight."

"How'd you know what to tell me
to help me with this?"

Mom smiled and hugged me and she gave me a kiss.

"You are a verb, Louis. That's just what you are.

Today you had focus, And it made you a star!

Being a verb is not easy, And it never will be.

But it isn't your fault, kid,

'cause you get it from me!"